5° & Other Poems

Books by
Nicholas Christopher

NICHOLAS CHRISTOPHER

5°

& Other

Poems

PENGUIN
POETS

PENGUIN BOOKS
Published by the Penguin Group
Penguin Books USA Inc., 375 Hudson Street,
New York, New York 10014, U.S.A.
Penguin Books Ltd, 27 Wrights Lane, London W8 5TZ, England
Penguin Books Australia Ltd, Ringwood, Victoria, Australia
Penguin Books Canada Ltd, 10 Alcorn Avenue,
Toronto, Ontario, Canada M4V 3B2
Penguin Books (N.Z.) Ltd, 182–190 Wairau Road,
Auckland 10, New Zealand

Penguin Books Ltd, Registered Offices:
Harmondsworth, Middlesex, England

First published in simultaneous hardcover and paperback
editions by Penguin Books 1995

10   9   8   7   6   5   4   3   2   1

LIBRARY OF CONGRESS CATALOGING IN PUBLICATION DATA
Christopher, Nicholas.
5° & other poems/Nicholas Christopher.
p.   cm.—(Penguin poets)
ISBN 0-670-85341-0 (hc.)
ISBN 0 14 058.718 7 (pbk.)
I. Title.   II. Title: Five degrees and other poems.
PS3553.H754A613   1995
811'.54—dc20   94–22934

Printed in the United States of America
Set in Bembo
Designed by Francesca Belanger

In Memory of
Robert Cullen

Acknowledgments

I am grateful to the John Simon
Guggenheim Memorial Foundation
for its generous support while I was
writing this book.

I would also like to thank
Richard Howard;
my editor, Dawn Seferian;
and my wife, Constance Christopher,
for their encouragement.

Contents

I. 5°

II. 25 Poems

I.

> > > > > > > > > > > > > > > >

5°

> > > > > > > > > > > > > > > >

> > > > > > > > > > > > > > > >

1.

Down the long avenues the north wind
doubles over the strongest men.

Everything has turned to iron:
buildings, pavement, the stunted trees.

Even the sky, from which lapis stars glint,
painful to the naked eye.

But for the clouds of their breath,
a man and his dog might be statues.

The pretzel vendor, his fingers brittle,
rakes his coals and sucks on a chip of ice.

In an archway, under a slanting hat,
a young woman is lighting a cigarette.

There is nothing in her eyes but the spit
of flame—amber enclosing a crimson thread—

as her shadow slips away, into a waiting car,
and the sidewalk swallows her up.

The smoke of her cigarette lingers,
coiling and floating across the street

intact—a halo that hovers all night
beneath the parapet of the church

where the angel with feverish eyes
snatches it up at dawn as the snow

begins to fall, and places it—heavy
as marble suddenly—behind his head.

2.

Charting points of longitude and latitude
on a satellite photograph of the moon
in a windowless room at a table of ice,
a man wearing the clothes he lost
while crossing the equator ten winters
ago coughs up a handful of coins.
On each coin is embossed the head
of a woman he knew who drowned
in the icy waters of a moonlit lake.
The coins are gold, with platinum
pinpoints in the woman's averted eyes.
On the other side is the back
of her head, the long hair
highlighted with strands of silver.
On both sides a nightingale
with snow dusting its wings
is hovering at her ear, singing.
A song the man himself might hum
on a bitterly cold night when the moon
drifts behind a frozen cloud and never emerges.

3.

In a letter to his brother Theo,
van Gogh wrote that he had earlier
that morning received the greatest
compliment ever paid him—by a doctor
who, upon examining him, remarked:
"I suppose you are an ironworker."
Van Gogh also mentioned that while in England
he applied for the position of "Evangelist
among the miners in the coal mines,
but they turned me down. . . ."

Coal and iron: the guts of the Earth,
scraped forth for furnaces and fires.
Brazil took its name from a redwood
whose bark reminded the conquistadors
of burning coals (*braise* in Portuguese).
How would van Gogh have painted in Brazil?
The choppy tropical colors slashing
the hills that rise up from the sea.
How would he have painted this street,
so cold the beams of headlights from cars
that passed hours ago remain frozen in midair.

4.

In the cemetery beside the river
the clipped grass has crystallized into glass.

A gravestone onto which a sailboat
is chiseled reads: LOTTE, LOST AT SEA.

Instead of hieroglyphics, an obelisk is covered
with the names of children who died in a hospital fire.

A mermaid and a centaur—cut from black marble—
adorn the entrance to the largest mausoleum,

solitary on a knoll behind iron bars and a padlocked gate.
From east to west, the snow drifts deeply,

obscuring the tortuous network of footpaths
that begin and end at the river, where

the blocks of ice, creaking and jostling,
never come to rest; from shore,

they resemble gravestones, endlessly
rearranging themselves in the fast water.

5.

Displayed in the coin shop window
below the Spanish doubloons and Flemish guilders,
in a row of talismans on felt cushions,
a gold disc deflects a ray of moonlight.

The sea-green card beneath it reads:
DISC EMPLOYED BY JOHN DEE (1527–1608)
WHO TRIED TO LEARN THE SECRETS
OF NATURE FROM ANGELS.

This same John Dee, court mathematician,
was a close friend to Sir Walter Ralegh
and Thomas Harriot, the first man
to map the lunar surface with a telescope.

The language Dee invented for communicating
with angels he called "Enochian."
His partner, Edward Kelley, was a medium
and a forger, whose ears had been lopped off.

Coins of the realm were Kelley's specialty.
Later, he was murdered in prison.
Dee died impoverished, reduced to casting
horoscopes in a provincial town.

He was reputed to be the model for Prospero.
His gold disc is ringed with concentric circles.
A sun at its center; a cross; four stone arches.
And hieroglyphics that hold the key
to what he learned from the angels,
which he never shared with anyone.

6.

Between the thick ice and the gray waters
of the lake there are seven inches
in which a man can breathe. So long as
he can tread water while tilting his head
upward at a forty-five-degree angle
indefinitely—until he freezes to death.

Harry Houdini, in Chicago to expose a pair
of bogus mediums, took time out
to have himself submerged in Lake Michigan
straitjacketed and weighted with chains
inside a padlocked, cast-iron milk container.
He escaped his restraints in thirty seconds,
but then could not locate the opening
that had been sawed in the ice for him;
and for two hours, wearing only a bathing
suit, he paddled slowly, searching
for the way out of that water cold
enough to kill a man in ten minutes.

When he emerged without physical injury,
not even frostbite, he attributed it
to his "mastery of all bodily controls."
Then he returned to his hotel suite,
and after dinner took a very hot bath,
followed by a very cold one—as was his custom.

7.

At the public library the gushing gutter water
has frozen in the gargoyles' mouths.
Arcs of silver shot through with black.
How long will it take to crack their iron jaws?

In the stacks of the subbasement,
in absolute darkness, on a shelf too high
to reach, there is a copy of Hesiod's
Works and Days, dusted with black snow,

in which can be found a definition
of the Iron Age of mankind that still applies:
"By day, they toil and grieve unceasingly;
by night, they waste away painfully and die."

The last and worst age of the world, Hesiod calls it,
in which men thrive on selfishness and deceit
until the gods destroy them in a single generation,
"causing babies to be born with graying hair."

After which their carcasses are carried off
by harpies and dropped the distance an anvil
might free-fall for ten days and nights,
into the subbasement of the underworld,

where griffons, centaurs, and hippogriffs
(who Ariosto claims hail from "iron mountains
far beyond the icebound seas") reign supreme.
And the gargoyles on the icy ledges gush fire.

8.

When the goddess Inanna made the long descent
to the underworld on a steep stairway—
the steps razor sharp and slippery—
a nightingale accompanied her,
hovering beside the thick plaits of her jet hair.

Inanna's Journey, a Sumerian text of the 18th
century B.C., survives in assorted tablets
and fragments of clay dug from the petrified
soil on the banks of the River Hubur—
"the man-devouring ditch of hell"—

which Inanna herself skirted en route
to the palace of lapis lazuli
within the seven walls of a concentric city
where the queen of the underworld sat
stark naked, white-eyed, on a throne of ice.

For a single season, Inanna (said to be
a model for Persephone) replaced the queen.
While she reclined on her throne, blinded
by the lapis stars spiked into the domed ceiling,
harsh winter gripped the earth above.

Her eyes were full moons.
Milky opals studded her breasts.
And damascene discs—iron impregnated
with gold—hung from her neck.
The nightingale that had never left her

sang into her ear, and in a dream within
her dream Inanna watched her own blue shadow
slip away and cross the vast plains
in swirling snow and ascend the mountains
planed by razor winds to the bare
. . . . .

> 10

orchard—the place of her birth—
where fruit the color of fire would soon
ripen on branches lined with nightingales.
All of whom, with silver-tipped wings
at rest, were singing a different song.

9.

Van Gogh wrote to Theo from Arles:
"I must also have a starry night with cypresses,
or perhaps surmounting a field of ripe corn. . . ."

Over which meteors would streak—
past Mercury, golden as a corn kernel,
and the Dog Star, haloed in blue—
to set the farm dogs barking.

The cypress, as he knew, is the oldest
variety of graveyard tree, cultivated
in Hell by Persephone herself (a former
corn goddess) beside the bottomless

pools from which the spirits drink
deeply and are never satisfied.
Cypresses lined the Public Garden
at Arles where van Gogh depicted them

vividly in blue, with silver highlights.
He liked to work there all afternoon,
munching a loaf of corn bread,
and then to doze until nightfall,

among flowers, on the hard benches.
When he painted his small room
on the other side of town, the bed
of cypress wood—lit up yellow

as the sun—dominated the canvas.
"I am in a continual fever of work,"
he wrote, completing five paintings in
five days. A year later, he shot himself
. . . . .

and was buried in a cypress coffin
in a cemetery between two cornfields
where the gravestones are visible
only in winter when the ground is bare.

Where the dogs, with frozen breath,
bay beneath iron trees
at the yellow moon that fills the sky.

10.

A man with a telescope on a marble runway
is shielding his eyes from the moon.
Like a match head, the Dog Star flares

over the island, famous for its cornfields
and its quarry: white marble so plenteous
it is used in lieu of concrete for everything

from the floors and stairways of the humblest
homes to this runway, hewn by a team of masons
and laid in place by farmers and fishermen

who wanted an air connection to the mainland.
Instead, the next year, they got the *Luftwaffe,*
first dropping paratroopers and then landing

transport planes with wings dusted by snow
crossing the Alps. For two years the Nazis
terrorized the island with armored cars,

flamethrowers, and attack dogs with iron teeth.
They built torture chambers in the town hall,
dynamited the church, and lopped off the mayor's ears.

They executed half the young men by firing squad
and flew the other half to Germany in dead of night.
When Allied warships appeared on the horizon

one morning, the Nazis fled by air and were
shot down over the sea. Survivors washed up
in the surf and the same farmers and fishermen

clubbed them to death with oars and shovels.
A salt-streaked obelisk marks the site,
with the names of the islanders murdered

. . . . .

during the occupation carved into its marble.
Meanwhile, the man with the telescope (the former
mayor, deaf and dumb, with a woolen cap

covering the stubs of his ears) is still
waiting for the plane to arrive bearing
the film company that plans to shoot *The Tempest*

on location. The actor who will play Prospero,
learning his lines at that moment, glances
through the window at the island, so flooded

with moonlight it seems to lie underwater,
that whiter-than-white runway shining like a beacon,
as it once shone for the Germans, who in Berlin,

where *The Merchant of Venice* was performed nightly,
flung copies of *The Tempest* into their bonfires
while the dogs, in packs, barked from the rooftops.

11.

"Iron occurs native in meteorites" (according to
the dictionary) "and is vital to biological processes."
Brought to the bloodstream from the farthest reaches

of the solar system. Only in meteorites is iron
found uncombined with other elements.
Tonight a meteor shower streams out of the chaotic

glitter of the stars. When stray dogs congregate
on the rooftops of abandoned tenements, the yellow
moon casts their shadows for an entire city block.

In ancient Egypt, Anubis, the dog-headed god, led
souls down a torchlit stairway to the underworld
and wore beads of meteoric iron around his neck.

Iron coins were placed under the tongues of the dead
in Crete to pay the stone-eyed ferryman Charon
for passage across the River Styx. In Rome, too,

where all gems and minerals beneath the earth's
surface were, by law, the property of Pluto,
god of the dead: iron and coal, opals and lapis.

Then, as now, grave robbers preferred aboveground
mausoleums: no digging; just a padlock to pick
and a casket to pry open. After which, shunning

the coin within its cage of clamped teeth, they
slipped bracelets and rings from skeletal hands
that shared a single trace element with meteorites:

iron, forged in the icy furnaces beyond Pluto—
beyond the Dog Star—where darkness is no longer
visible, and even the gods of the dead fear to go.

12.

Flanked by stone owls, a woman leans against
an iron gate, clutching a halved pomegranate,
rolling its seeds around her tongue.
Her eyes, flecked like mica, reflect the stars.
When she speaks, her lips do not move,
her voice never wavers—
like Persephone, whose name in Greek means
"she who brings destruction."
(In Latin, Proserpina: "the fearful one.")
The falling snow avoids her,
and the sudden gusts that sweep down the avenue
between rows of buildings so steep
not even a vine can climb them.
Striking a match, she holds the teardrop
flame to the pomegranate,
which comes alive, scarlet as a human heart,
with moist, glittering chambers.
Then the wind carries away her shadow
and ruffles the owls' feathers and whistles
the snow from the keyhole of the gate
that is never locked, but which only she can open.

13.

In 1910 Houdini was the first man to fly
an airplane successfully in Australia.
It was a biplane, which he bought in France
and took with him to Melbourne on a ship.
During the entire voyage, he was seasick,
yet he spent all his free time
in the cargo hold, in darkness,
sitting at the controls of his plane.
He had *Houdini* painted on the fuselage
and wings in large red letters.

In Melbourne he gave two performances nightly.
He made a full-grown elephant disappear onstage.
He caused the top hat of a man
in the back row to fill with gold coins.
He had himself submerged, straitjacketed
and handcuffed, in a tank of ice water.
Then he would leave his wife
at their hotel and hurry to a desert
airstrip to spend the night in his plane.
He kept this up for weeks, barely sleeping,
while waiting for the weather to clear.

On the evening of February 18th, a huge crowd
watched him leap manacled from Queen's Bridge
into the muddy waters of the Yarra River.
Moments later, a corpse floated to the surface.
Believing this was Houdini, the crowd panicked,
and when Houdini himself, free of manacles,
rose to the surface triumphantly,
he was so startled by this apparition
that he was unable to swim and had to be hauled
forcibly into a rowboat by his attendants.

Finally, on March 16th, under cloudless skies,
he took off in his plane, circled

the field, and made a perfect landing.
He completed three flights that day,
covering seven miles at an altitude of ninety feet.
At each stop, cheering crowds greeted him.
In April, he made four more flights
before crashing outside Sydney on the 22nd.
He walked away from the wrecked plane unscathed.
And unshaken. Telling his wife that over
the previous month he had not slept at all.

"I now seem to have lost the habit," he said.
To his journal he confided that history
would now remember him, not as a magician,
but as an aviation pioneer.
During the entire voyage home, he was seasick.
He never flew again.

14.

A nightingale disappears into a mirror
in a vacant lot deep with snow.

The mirror reflects nothing:
not the steep buildings on three sides

or the parked cars with iced windows
or the frozen clouds suspended from stars.

In the distance, a lone dog barks.
Another dog, even farther away, replies.

And then another, very faint.
They form the few audible links

in a long chain stretching away
to the windswept plains where lapis

highways connect ruined cities,
where the mirrors do not reflect,

but only conceal, such things as
this nightingale saw before streaking

out of the mirror with every black feather
turned white, never to sing again.

15.

An angel is signing his name in blue light
on a black wall. Recording his history,
over thirteen centuries, on the head of a pin.
Writing in a language known only to other angels,
but with such variations as to confuse even them.

The fragments that will survive are being spirited
away by fugitive translators who will languish
in underground prisons until they die.

In the courtyard of one such prison,
modeled after the innermost circle of Dante's
Inferno, a statue of a frozen, bearded man

is planted headfirst in the ice, like Satan
who is to remain in this position for all
eternity after being hurled down from Heaven.

He has three faces, six eyes, and three mouths
from which dark blood issues. For recreation,
the prisoners are allowed to climb in his beard.

In London, Newgate Prison was rebuilt in 1780,
following the blueprint of a fantastical drawing
by Piranesi, executed thirty years earlier.

Another instance of life imitating art,
which, contrary to popular misconceptions,
is not the exception but the rule.

As van Gogh knew, in his final days at Arles,
moving into a house called the "Yellow House"
when he began painting in yellow.

And Shakespeare, who understood that the hard
facts he pillaged from Plutarch were prefigured
in myths—the wellspring of history—

. . . . .

which is why the *Parallel Lives* begins
(apologetically) with Theseus and Romulus,
founders of Athens and Rome in those remote ages

of "prodigies and fables, the province of poets."
The stuff the angels have transcribed for us,
only a fraction of which—like the number
of waking moments a prisoner actually forgets
he is imprisoned—will be deciphered.

16.

On the other side of the world,
as on the other side of a dream,
the surface of the Sahara Desert is 140°.

In the fourth book of his *Histories*
Herodotus catalogs the tribes who inhabited
"the great belt of sand beyond the regions

where wild beasts are found," including
the Psylli, who declared war on the south wind
(after it dried up their water supply)

and, marching all night, were buried alive
in sand by the wind; and the Atarantes,
"the only people in the world to do without

names," who screeched and heaped curses
upon the sun as it rose, trailing ashes
on the horizon. Other tribes he mentions

are the Maxyes, "dog-headed men" who dyed
their bodies red; and the Gyzantes,
who did the same, and ate flying snakes

and monkeys, and also perfected a way
to make honey without bees; and off the desert
coast, on an island called Cyrauis, a tribe

of women who lived by a lake "and dipped
feathers smeared with pitch into the muddy
lake bottom and brought up gold dust"

which they sprinkled on their hair
before going into battle or making love.
These tribes shared the same god.

. . . . .

From a vast underworld, he commanded legions
of ants in silver armor whose sole task
was to fetch him the dead; in a single

night they could break down and transport
an entire body through their tunnels.
The god himself was transparent, composed

of a substance from the other side of the world,
so cold it could tear the skin from a man's flesh.
Ice:

when the god opened his arms at dawn
to welcome the dead, it melted into
a swift, deep river and carried them away.

17.

The fire at the foundling hospital raged all night.
Jets of water from the fire hoses froze in midair.
Blinded by the vapors of their breath,
the firemen inched up ladders into the smoke.

A nurse with a child clinging to her back
crept along a ledge on all fours
and disappeared in a gust of snow.

All of the foundlings were lost again—
this time with no one to find them but the dogs
who were led sniffing through the ashes at dawn,
whose howls echoed beyond the river

where blocks of ice rolled downstream
under the stars that are always burning
in the sky, but can only be found at night.

18.

John Davis, explorer and navigator, died the night
The Tempest was first performed in London.
As a young man, he sailed deep into the polar

regions, along uncharted sea lanes, on the bark
Moonlight, in search of the Northwest Passage.
Near the Arctic Circle, he saw a mountain

of gold on a distant headland, which he named
Mount Ralegh, after his friend Sir Walter,
whose obsession with El Dorado, the elusive

city of gold in the Amazon jungle, was well known.
But Davis's concerns were with iron, not gold.
He recorded that the people he encountered

slept on their feet, were left-handed,
and (like the white-eyed dogs that pulled
their sleds) able to see for miles in the darkness.

Also, that they craved all things iron—
hooks, knives, buttons, anchors—
which they were not above stealing openly.

Their word for iron, he added, was *Aoh.*
Davis befriended these people, but thought
them "witches," capable of "many enchantments,"

including their ability to kindle fires
in howling wind and to remain neck-deep in icy
waters, "amongst the fishes," for whole days.

He wondered at their diet, for "they consume all
their meat raw, and live most upon fish, and drink
salt water, and eat grass and ice with delight."
. . . . .

Continuing northward, Davis encountered an iceberg
so huge ("with bays and capes and high cliffs")
that it took him two weeks to sail past it.

Then a mysterious illness spread among his men:
overnight, their hair turned white and, scalded
by fever, they lost all desire for sleep.

Violent storms and high seas racked the ship.
Those who didn't drown, or freeze to death, took
their own lives. Davis survived, and with a skeleton

crew pushed on through sheets of blinding snow.
Months later, when they brought the *Moonlight*
back to Portsmouth, he remained on board, alone,

and in the darkness of his cabin made his final
entry in the ship's log, writing in a clear hand
that he had dropped anchor in Iceland, and Greenland,

and then a country no European had ever laid eyes on,
whose coordinates he noted carefully.
He called it Desolation.

19.

In October, 1888, Paul Gauguin joined van Gogh
in the Yellow House at Arles and dreamt of
the desert after sketching the flora of Martinique
on a tablecloth for his companion after dinner.

For six nights he had the same dream, and on
the seventh woke to find van Gogh standing,
fast asleep, beside his bed with a pistol.
The next morning, Gauguin executed his first

canvas in that house: two girls picking
mangoes near a stream, under the gaze
of a red horse tethered to a banyan tree.
A single element of his recurrent dream

appeared in the lower-left-hand corner
of this painting, beneath the dipping arm
of a lush fern: a shiny, long-legged insect
unknown in those days, but identifiable now

as the Saharan silver ant. In his dream,
hundreds of them were marching in lockstep
on the scorching sand, just as the Nazis'
armored legions would one day cross North Africa.

Gauguin's posthumous admirers naturally thought
the ant to be of a tropical species.
Gauguin himself, who had never visited
the desert, nearly painted over the ant,

he confided to his journal, until van Gogh
casually mentioned that he, too, had once
encountered such an insect in a dream.
Set not in the tropics, or the desert, but in

. . . . .

a kind of hell beneath that very house, down
steep steps, where men chained to a wall under
hot lamps screamed while silver-helmeted
(antlike) soldiers lacerated their backs.

During the occupation, the Yellow House
would serve as headquarters for the Gestapo
in Arles, and it was in the basement
that they conducted their interrogations.

"Leave the ant in," van Gogh advised, fifty-one
years earlier, "as the emissary to your paradise
from the inferno we call Europe." And Gauguin did.

20.

A white house against a black mountain
against a white sky from which
silver snowflakes blow down one by one.

A woman with long black hair steps
from the door and brushes the topmost
twig on an ice-coated maple so that

its branches tinkle like bells,
startling a nightingale on the roof
who swoops away, threading the iron trees.

The woman crosses a field to a well.
She breaks the ice on its surface
by dropping a stone, and as she lowers

a bucket hears a pack of dogs approaching
suddenly from deep in the forest.
The snowfall thickens, sticking to her lips,

as she realizes the dogs will reach
her before she can reach the house.
Before she can even draw the bucket,

which she continues to raise, one
hand at a time, on its frozen rope.

21.

Houdini, who had once escaped a steel-lined
Siberian prison van, and the maximum-security
cell that held President Garfield's assassin,
and even (like Jonah) the carcass of a whale
in which he had been sewn fast by surgeons,
could not escape death, which surprised him

in a Detroit hospital across from an ironworks
where he was pronounced dead of a ruptured
appendix on Halloween Day, 1926. In the last
minute of his life, his temperature plunged
from 104° to 84°. "That was his soul
leaving the body," his wife said to the doctor.

He was buried in Wisconsin in a bronze casket
which he had used in his final performance:
airtight and waterproof, it was submerged
in a glass tank filled with ice water,
Houdini handcuffed and manacled within.
A curtain was drawn over the tank.
Two, three, four minutes passed, and there

was no sign of him. Women screamed.
Someone pulled the fire alarm. . . .
It always went like this. Until Houdini
sauntered down the aisle from the back
of the theater and opened the curtain,
revealing the tank, empty of water, to be
filled with gold coins and the casket gone.

He had promised his wife he would send
her a message from beyond the grave.
But despite countless séances with mediums
on five continents, no message ever came.
The bust on his mausoleum was vandalized,
but his grave was left undisturbed.
So it caused a commotion one Halloween

. . . . .

many years after his death when the bronze
casket turned up in a Manhattan warehouse
in a cache of his other stage props.
Corroded and earth-stained, it was pried open,
and a single gold coin was discovered inside.
A woman's head, with platinum pinpoints in
her averted eyes, was embossed on the coin.

The coin was sent to the police laboratory,
but by dawn its face was smooth: the woman's
head had receded back into the gold. The casket
languished for years among the props; when it
disappeared one winter night, the temperature in
the warehouse plummeted and, despite all changes
of season, to this day remains fixed at exactly 5°.

22.

The Hyperboreans—"people beyond the North Wind"—
according to Diodorus Siculus, inhabited an island
from which the moon "appears to be but a little
distance from the earth and to have upon it
prominences, like those of the earth," easily visible.

Some believed this island to be England, home
of Thomas Harriot, the first lunar cartographer,
and botanist to Ralegh's Virginia expedition
in 1586, two thousand years after the Hyperboreans
disappeared from the annals of history.

Herodotus mentions a tribe even farther north,
of one-eyed men and griffons who guard hoards
of gold in ice fortresses and "make war upon the ice"
during their long winters when "the ground is frozen
iron hard," requiring, not water, but fire to soften it.

Long before John Davis plied Arctic waters, word
had reached these two Greek historians, who had
never ventured north of the Black Sea, that there
was such a people, skilled in fishing through ice
and hunting in darkness, who slept on their feet.

The snow around them so thick, Herodotus reported,
that it was described to him as an "unceasing wind
filled with feathers"; and Diodorus (who had never
seen snow) referred to it as a "great cloud shredded
by the North Wind." Today, hurtling northward in

our hearts at breakneck speed, we have outdistanced
all previous tribes, walking the planet's starry
rim like a tightrope with the pocked moon close
enough to touch. It was another Englishman,
Sir Thomas Browne (born when Davis and Harriot
. . . . .

were old men), who chose for his meditation on
death and the underworld, *Hydriotaphia* (*Urne-Buriall*)—
which is dense with digressions on the psychology
of arches and obelisks, and astral nomenclature
(with special attention to the "Dogge-Starre"),

and the fact that Roman colonists in Britain,
when they left off torturing and dispossessing
the resident Saxons, also taught them the art
of minting coins—a fittingly Hyperborean epigraph,
icy in its simplicity, by yet another citizen

of the sunny south: the line of verse Sextus
Propertius, in 15 B.C., had etched onto
the urn that would hold his ashes—white as
mountain snow—in the catacombs of Rome,
"See, I am now what can be lifted with five fingers."

23.

The itinerant magician working the night
train wears a costume black down
one side and white down the other—
silk, with hexagons across the chest.
There is a silver bucket at his feet
into which coins may be tossed
while he performs coin tricks.
Making them disappear in midair,
or spinning them on his fingertips
and transforming them from gold
to iron, to gold again.
An ice chip under his tongue,
he sings the song Ariel sang
while Prospero's hounds—elusive
as smoke—barked from the wings.
Then, after blindfolding himself,
wearing a white glove and a black one,
he juggles six pomegranates.
Beneath the downturned smile
penciled onto his whiteface,
his own smile is a zigzag lifted
from a map of the snow country
through which this train is speeding
along tracks of ice—not iron—
that are melting in its wake.

24.

The polestar (Polaris) during the Dark Ages
was called the "Nail of the Heavens"—
an iron nail hammered into the frozen sky.

Between this nail and the center of the Underworld—
an onyx cave whose domed ceiling was spiked
with stars—was stretched the *axis mundi,* like a harp
string, sounding the solitary note of Creation.

Only a single piece of land lay along this axis:
an island of iron boulders from which St. Brendan
the Voyager set sail for America a century

before Columbus, but ended up exploring
the Canary Islands with his party of monks,
who spoke in tongues and traded the native
inhabitants iron pebbles for ripe pomegranates.

In demonstrating the wonders of his faith,
St. Brendan caused a waterfall to flow upward,
and—like Prospero—called forth dead men

from their graves and darkened the sun at noon.
(Could it have been St. Brendan, rather than
John Dee or Walter Ralegh, who was the first,
most prodigious, model for Prospero?)

The number of his conversions remains cloudy,
but we know that one of his monks bolted
and remained behind on the westernmost island

of Hierro (Iron), hiding in a cave, living on
spiders, lizards, and the juice of sea grapes,
a Caliban crouched behind a curtain of foliage
who, watching his shipmates set sail for Ireland,
. . . . .

heard a single plucked note reverberating
in his ears. And when the rough sea was empty—
the breakers streaming a spray of gems off the rocks—

he crawled down to the beach and rolled in sand
black as coal and howled at that one star
nailed fast among a million wavering lights.

25.

The *Voyager 2* satellite, launched from Florida
on a starry night in 1977, atop a booster rocket
propelled by liquid nitrogen (optimum temperature

at combustion: 5°), tonight sailed past Pluto
and its lone moon, Charon—named after
the ferryman who, with Cerberus the 3-headed

dog, is gatekeeper to the underworld—
leaving our solar system behind. It was
the *Voyager* that transmitted the first close-up

photographs of Saturn and Neptune, and then
Uranus and two of its icy moons, Ariel
and Miranda, which it had taken the satellite

fifteen years to reach. In 1957, the Russians
launched *Sputnik II* from Star City (a space
center erected on the Siberian permafrost)

with a single occuptant, the dog Laika, a mixed
breed from Central Asia who was in his prime—
highly intelligent, good-natured and trusting

to a fault. And after he had told them
(electrodes attached to his body and sensors
implanted in his brain) all they wanted

to know about weightlessness, motion sickness,
and the effects of gamma rays on a mammal
above the protection of the Ozone layer,

they allowed him to spin out of the ionosphere
and hurtle toward the outer planets, where he
died a slow death when his supply of food,
. . . . .

> 38

water, and air ran out. Perfectly preserved
in the vacuum of his iron compartment,
Laika also flew past Ariel and Miranda,

past Pluto and Charon, into interstellar
space, where if he continues traveling
at his last recorded speed for 10,000 years—

at which time the tilt of the Earth's axis
will have shifted 5°, plunging it into
another Ice Age—Laika will reach Sirius,

the Dog Star, whose sapphire rays,
pinpointed in his black eyes, will enter
his body and flood it with light.

26.

"Iron" in Sumerian means "metal from heaven."

The iron comprising 5% of the earth's crust
arrived here as meteors during the Ice Age.
When the iron core of a neutron star—

a steely sphere with a smooth surface—
collapses, it sounds a tremendous clang,
like a cymbal a thousand times the size

of the Sun, and rolls a sonic wave through
deep space, followed by a stream (as from
a cornucopia) of gold, silver, tin, and iron—

millions of tons of these metals buckshotting
into the cosmos while the former star flattens
into a black hole. The particle spray off

a single iron pellet of this buckshot may
after many years' travel enter our atmosphere
as a meteor shower, leveler of mountains

and cities, feared by ancient man, who,
regardless of the gods he worshipped,
always kept one eye trained on the heavens.

There was, in fact, a city named Iron (cited in
the Book of Joshua) in the mountains of northern
Palestine that disappeared without a trace.

Iron, with a hard *r,* is the Hebrew word for "fear."

27.

Stray dogs are baying at the edge of the roof.
For every vacant lot there is a blue streetlight.

In the razor wind two men in steel helmets
are welding the iron steps of the fire escape.

The snow swirls through the sparks of their torches.
Then it swallows the men.

Baring icy teeth, the dogs race down the fire escape,
single file for six stories, and beyond.

Through the buckled pavement, along a freezing
zigzag to the underworld, where they retrieve

the bones of the dead who once occupied this tenement:
a burned-out building at the city limits

to which the welders were sent to repair
a fire escape no one but the dogs will use,

piling a pyramid of bones on the sagging
roof until it gives way.

28.

An ancient lapidary observed that onyx reflected
the shadows rather than the images of things.
And Pliny in his *Natural History* quotes Sudines:
"In onyx one finds a white band resembling a human
fingernail," and goes on to extol the beauty of
jasper onyx, which "is speckled, as if with falling snow."

By the time of her ascent from the underworld,
when the goddess emerged at the entrance
to the steep stairway with its razor steps that only
she could climb, her full-moon eyes had turned to onyx,
black with the shadows that had entered them down
among the dead, who were packed shoulder to shoulder

in cavernous halls, dancing their slow, concentric dances.
In fact, "onyx" is derived from the Greek for "fingernail."
The crescents rising from the cuticles of Inanna's
fingernails were luminous as moons over a polar sea.
But only a sliver of the full moon remained
discernible in her eyes as she peered through

the swirling snow, across the plain that divides
the mountains of iron from the mountains of ice,
trying to separate images from their shadows,
to distinguish the living from the dead.

29.

Eight months before he died of cardiac arrest,
and thirteen years after van Gogh's suicide,
Paul Gauguin, exhausted, impoverished, and alone
on the tiny island of Hiva-Oa (5° south latitude)
in the Marquesas chain, was still writing to friends
in Paris of how he taught van Gogh to paint in yellow:
"At first, yellow suns on a yellow surface . . .
sun-effects over sun-effects in full sunlight."

In Arles, between Halloween and Christmas, 1888,
van Gogh and Gauguin lived in a bright yellow house.
The only painting van Gogh sold in his lifetime,
Red Vineyard, was executed under its roof, dedicated
to Gauguin—a canvas awash in chrome yellow.
At the same time, Gauguin painted van Gogh painting
        sunflowers.
Van Gogh was on the verge of a breakdown, and Gauguin,
his "iron companion," was spooked by his sleepwalking,

his ravings, even his bad cooking—done according
to color ("mixed like paints"), not taste.
All of which came to an abrupt halt one night
in the Public Garden, among the cypresses, when van Gogh
burst upon Gauguin with an open razor that later he
turned on himself. At which point, badly shaken, Gauguin
boarded a train for Paris, and went on to Brittany.
The previous day, van Gogh had written to Theo:

"Altogether I think that either Gauguin will
definitely go, or else definitely stay."
And: "Because I hoped to live with Gauguin, I made
a decoration for his studio. Nothing but sunflowers."
And it was sunflowers, not wreaths, that were placed
around van Gogh's coffin at his funeral.
In 1903, on Hiva-Oa, Gauguin ordered sunflower seeds
from France, grew them patiently, and painted still lifes

. . . . .

of the flowers exactly as van Gogh had arranged them
in his room in the Yellow House. In his journal
he recalled those sunflowers that stood in a yellow vase
on a yellow table, inundated by a "yellow sun that shone
through the yellow curtains." But in the room in which
he would die, with only his dog beside the bed, as far
from France as a ship could take him, his legs raw
with ulcers and ants overrunning the floor, there were

no sunflowers and no light, and despite the jungle heat,
his heart was contracting like ice in his chest.
Fastened to his easel was an unfinished canvas,
Breton Village Under the Snow,
with these words scrawled on the back in yellow:
"To draw freely is not to lie to oneself."

30.

At the end of *The Tempest,* between promising Miranda's
hand in marriage and routing the rebellious Caliban
with the assistance of Ariel and his hounds (whose
names, for once, are revealed: Mountain, Fury, Tyrant
& Silver), Prospero conjures up, as a wedding present,
a masque featuring three ancient goddesses, including
Demeter, protectress of cornfields, who curiously
(under the circumstances) laments the marriage of her
own daughter, Persephone, once a sunburnt, carefree
girl like Miranda and now the queen of the underworld.

When the play is performed by a visiting troupe
of actors on the island where the ruins of Demeter's
temple, perched above a fertile valley, serve as
an open-air theater, the audience, sitting raptly
in moonlight, consists of fishermen and farmers.
Most notably, a group of corn reapers, still dusty
from their labors, who applaud during the masque
when some Reapers, in black, with sickles bright
as quarter-moons strapped to their backs, dance
with the Nymphs of Spring while Ariel, reclined
atop a column, his eyes roaming the stars of remote
galaxies, plays a wavering tune on his iron flute.

By dawn, the troupe has left the island, with
the exception of the actress who played Miranda.
Still in costume (a white gown girdled with lapis
seashells), she has remained at the temple, on a block
of marble beside Demeter's broken statue, peeling
a pomegranate and waiting for the sun to rise over
the yellow fields. Her jet hair is plaited loosely,
and there is a restive dog at her feet, who at first
light leads her down the stone steps that spiral
around the hillside, past the sleeping town, and then
down another, darker stairway to a cypress grove,

a shuttered room with an onyx bed on which she dreams of drowning men frozen fast in an icy sea, and a magician clothed in the robes of death who refuses to set them free.

31.

Of the eighteen cities called Alexandria that Alexander
the Great founded or renamed, from the Sahara Desert
to the Arctic Circle, only the first, in Egypt, remains
standing after two millennia. According to Plutarch,

after Alexander proclaimed himself pharaoh, he
personally chose the site of the city, overruling
his architects, because of a dream in which an old
man directed him to the windy headland at the Nile

delta opposite the island of Pharos. The Arab
historian Mas'ûdî, insisting that the new pharaoh
was also a magician, reports that when the city's
foundations were being laid, "savage monsters" emerged

from the sea at night and tore down everything
that had been built by day. No watchmen, not even
crack troops posted on the beach, could deter them.
So Alexander had a box constructed, casket-shaped,

with sheets of glass on three sides, in which he
stretched out with paper and stylus. Weighted
with iron, the box was lowered to the seafloor,
where Alexander observed the monsters, who had

human torsos and the heads of beasts. After sketching
them, he ordered his sculptors to produce exact
likenesses in marble and position them along the shore.
When the sea monsters next appeared, and confronted

their own graven images, they plunged terrified back
into the sea and were never seen again. Mas'ûdî also
tells us of Alexander's little-known exploits as
an aviator, explaining that when he traveled into the far
. . . . .

north Alexander built a "flying machine" in order to avoid
the icebound seas: a pair of griffons was chained to
a basket in which Alexander sat and raised a piece of meat
on a stick above their heads, inducing them to flight.

Pausanias notes that the icy water of the Styx, capable of
"dissolving glass and crystal, bronze, silver and gold,"
can only be contained by a mule's hoof. Which is
reputedly how it was served up to Alexander during

his fatal drinking bout in Babylon. He was embalmed by
Egyptian members of his court, who then spent twelve years
building a proper chariot—temple-sized, adorned with golden
griffons—to carry his body into the desert for burial,

as he had demanded. Instead, they took him to Alexandria,
where he was placed in the same glass casket in which
he had been submerged to sketch the sea monsters.
And there he lay, a coin minted with his own image

under his tongue, on display for three hundred years.
Until his casket disappeared without a trace on a night
so cold that in the bustling city which had sprung from
his dreams, blocks of ice were seen floating on the Nile.

32.

Refracted by frozen clouds, the moon's
rays sweep the granite towers
and deflect off their black windows.
Behind each square of thick glass
a body reclines in sleep,
deaf to the wind-rattled streets.

Hesiod writes that the north wind makes
"the old man bend, round-shouldered as a wheel,"
and slicks the ice under his feet.
Stone Age men, grinding pigments from cobalt,
painted themselves, dog-headed, electric,
on stalactites in their caves.

In *The Book of Jubilees,* a heretical version
of Genesis flung into bonfires in the Dark Ages,
an Angel of Ice is mentioned, but not named.
Whereas Gabriel, the Angel of the North,
is one of only two angels named—
and praised—in the Old Testament.

He is said to preside over Paradise,
and to have leveled Sodom and Gomorrah.
Mohammed wrote that Gabriel "of the 140 pairs of wings"
dictated the Koran to him, *sura* by *sura.*
And Luke (1:26) credits him, not the Holy Ghost,
with begetting Jesus upon the Virgin Mary.

When Gabriel descends from the north
with his staff of ice that extends
from the polestar to the center of the earth,
the frigid wind howls from his lips,
whipped up by his beating wings,
and doubles over the strongest men.

33.

At the South Pole the blue ice fields are combed
each year for meteorites—entombed since they plunged

from the sky in the late Pliocene epoch, before human
history—that surface when the wind, like a razor,

scrapes away another layer of ice. Some are the debris
of two asteroids that collided near the Sun;

others are fragments of the Moon, blasted loose by
larger meteors and hurled earthward; still others,

in the same way, were sheared off the mountains of Mars;
but the most common meteorites in Antarctica—

which men still explore as they would another planet—
are stellar. Early explorers used the stars to navigate

unknown seas, and with remote islanders bartered
iron (fashioned into nails and fishhooks) that arrived,

via meteorites, from those same stars. Tonight, stars
as far away in time as they are in space are exploding,

shooting off chunks of iron at the speed of sound
that may one day—as "falling stars," trailing fire—

reach the Earth and penetrate the polar ice.
In 1656, soon after Galileo had laid the foundations

of modern astronomy, the mathematician Athanasius Kircher
in his book *Voyage Ecstatique* came to a similar conclusion

regarding the origins of meteors. "The Sun," he wrote,
"is peopled with angels of fire swimming in seas of light
. . . . .

around a volcano from which pour myriads of meteors."
When the Sun flares out, and the Earth turns to ice,

will those angels retain their luminous form and seek out
another star, or merge with the darkness, cold as iron?

34.

A man in a windowless room at a table of ice
has pushed aside his map of the moon and is dreaming
of a ghost ship, laden with gold, flying a frozen flag.

Thomas Browne, discussing lunar cartography, agreed
with the Stoics' assertion "that the souls of wise men
dwelt about the Moon, and those of fools wandered the Earth."

As a boy, he witnessed the death of Walter Ralegh.
The latter, awaiting the executioner's ax
in the Tower of London, completed the first (and last)

volume of his *History of the World,* breaking off
in 168 B.C. with the rise of the Roman Empire.
And with these words: "It is therefore Death alone

that can suddenly make man to know himself."
Convicted on charges of blasphemy and sedition,
Ralegh was in truth condemned by a kangaroo court

for failing to discover El Dorado, the city of gold,
on his final, ill-fated voyage to the New World.
During which his reading consisted of Pliny the Elder

and Diodorus Siculus' *History,* in which he specially noted
the description of Orpheus' descent to the underworld,
accompanied by nightingales, to serenade Persephone

and of the "helmet of invisibility" worn by her husband
that allowed him to visit the sunlit world unseen.
Just as death today moves among us at all times,

touching our shoulders, our eyelids, our lips,
until it takes us firmly by the hand—or the throat—
when suddenly we run out of days and nights.
. . . . .

Ralegh stated that all explorers must die of heartbreak.
Among his many pursuits were charting the lunar surface
and discovering what elements might comprise the soul.

Pliny referred him to Hipparchus, "who established
that our souls are particles of heavenly fire."
But in his journal Ralegh tacitly disagreed and listed

two elements of which he was certain: ice and iron,
reduced to powder and then ground fine.
The rest, he said, he would leave to others to find.

35.

At 5°, nearing zero, things are speeding up.
The snow is falling fast, burying the parked cars.

It is the iron hour before dawn.
A dog snaps his leash and races under the trees.

The truck that spreads salt is idling without a driver,
its frozen headlights turning the corner at a right angle.

The pretzel vendor's cart creaks on bent wheels
as he inches up the avenue, into the north wind.

A young woman hurries from a basement apartment
with a cluster of grapes the color of hot coals.

Hat aslant, eyes slits, she pauses beneath
the angel who prowls the parapet of the church.

Her shadow flows the wrong way—toward the streetlight.
One by one she drops those grapes down a grate

(where coins are fished up by children) and for
ten days and nights they fall, past the ashes

of all the fires that ever burned, past the tree
of ice in which countless nightingales perch

but do not sing, streaking into the underworld,
its domed, moonless sky, where they burn like stars.

II.

> > > > > > > > > > > > > > >

25

> > > > > > > > > > > > > > >

Poems

> > > > > > > > > > > > > > >

Hibiscus Tea

The cup of tea in the dying man's room trembled
with each blow of the laborer's hammer.
Across the road, by the dusty trees,
they were splitting stone in fierce sunlight.
The shadows of the men clotting

with the shadows of the trees;
the stone to be hewn for an aqueduct
that would relieve future droughts;
the tea, red as blood, gradually
overflowing the cup and filling its saucer.

And the man, dead before the sun sank
behind the broken teeth of the mountains,
confessing no sins and tasting blood on his lips
when he parted them for the last time
to complain of a sudden, deep thirst.

The Quiñero Sisters, 1968

Against the flares of falling stars
over the man-made lake
in the middle of which we were reclining
on a creaking raft, they sang a wicked
duet of "Be My Baby," swaying and dipping
in their identical white bikinis,
snapping their wrists like The Ronettes.
The water dripping from their hair.
They were twins who were not identical.
Victoria's eyes a deep blue.
Virginia's a pale brown.
(A genetic marvel, as I knew
from my biology texts.)
Virginia was a soprano.
Victoria, with her husky whisper, a contralto.
In the moonlight, their faces shone.
Lips gleaming. Teeth flashing like silver.
To our left, in the deep darkness,
the waterfall roared; one night in June
a rowboat had strayed over those falls
and two friends of ours were drowned,
their naked bodies, tightly embraced,
dredged up the next morning a mile downriver.
Now, on the last night of the summer,
we had come in a borrowed, baby-blue
convertible, driving fast along the mountain
roads, the high-beam lights picking up
the red eyes of animals crouched
in the high grass—Victoria, Virginia,
her boyfriend, who was also named Nick,
and me, behind the wheel. The other Nick
was about to go to Vietnam, and I was
about to enter college, and side by side
on the raft we were passing a bottle
of red wine while the girls sang.
We were seventeen, except for Nick,

a carpenter's apprentice, who had turned
eighteen in July and been drafted in August.
And five months later, in a library in
Cambridge in dead of winter, I would see
his name listed among the dead in a newspaper—
killed in action outside Da Nang.
But that night, under the sky riddled
with stars, with the wind licking our lips
and the water lapping softly beneath
the raft, he and I (two boys with the same
name) never took our eyes off the Quiñero
sisters (twins who didn't even look
like sisters), revolving their open
palms in rhythmical circles, as if
they were trying to erase the night.
Oh, since the day I saw you,
I have been waiting for you,
You know I will adore you, till Eternity
They harmonized in and around the melody,
until, hands on hips and hair flying,
they threw their heads back and held
the last sweet note. And held it. For hours,
it seemed, while the moon slid through
the clouds, and bats skimmed the water,
and the fish jumped, and then, reluctantly,
we left that raft, moored to the muddy lake
bottom, and two by two swam back to shore.
Virginia and Nick hurried up the hill,
and Victoria and I laid a blanket under
the trees, on the grass bank, and peeled off
our suits. Shuddering now, with the insects
buzzing around us like static, she opened
her arms and pulled me on top of her.
Ten years later, after two busted marriages,
her sister would open her wrists
and slip into a tub of blood-warm water.

And a year after that, to the day, Victoria
would be killed in a car crash, beside
a man she met at a party, who crossed
the double line into oncoming traffic
with a bottle cradled between his knees.
But when I held her that night,
breathing in the scent of her hair,
I felt her fingers dance along my spine
and her eyelashes moisten as she whispered
in my ear—I can hear it clearly—
her voice even then falling away from me,
"Be my baby now...."

Terminus

Here is a piece of required reading
at the end of our century
the end of a millennium that began with the crusades

The transcript of an interview
between a Red Cross doctor
and a Muslim girl in Bosnia
twelve years old
who described her rape by men
calling themselves soldiers
different men every night one after the other
six seven eight of them
for a week
while she was chained by the neck
to a bed in her former schoolhouse
where she saw her parents and her brothers
have their throats slit and tongues cut out
where her sister-in-law
nineteen years old and nursing her baby
was also raped night after night
until she dared to beg for water
because her milk had run dry
at which point one of the men
tore the child from her arms
and as if he were "cutting an ear of corn"
(the girl's words)
lopped off the child's head
with a hunting knife
tossed it into the mother's lap
and raped the girl again
slapping her face
smearing it with her nephew's blood
and then shot the mother
who had begun to shriek
with the head wide-eyed in her lap

shoving his gun into her mouth
and firing twice

All of this recounted to the doctor
in a monotone
a near whisper in a tent
beside an icy river
where the girl had turned up frostbitten
wearing only a soiled slip
her hair yanked out
her teeth broken

All the history you've ever read
tells you this is what men do
this is only a sliver of the reflection
of the beast
who is a fixture of human history
and the places you heard of as a boy
that were his latest stalking grounds
Auschwitz Dachau Treblinka
and the names of their dead
and their numberless dead whose names have vanished
each day now find their rolls swelled
with kindred souls
new names new numbers
from towns and villages
that have been scorched from the map

1993 may as well be 1943
and it should be clear now
that the beast in his many guises
the flags and vestments
in which he wraps himself
and the elaborate titles he assumes
can never be outrun
. . . . .

As that girl with the broken teeth
loaded into an ambulance
strapped down on a stretcher
so she wouldn't claw her own face
will never outrun him
no matter where she goes
solitary or lost in a crowd
the line she follows
however straight or crooked
will always lead her back to that room
like the chamber at the bottom
of Hell in the Koran
where the Zaqqūm tree grows
watered by scalding rains
"bearing fruit like devils' heads"

In not giving her name
someone has noted at the end
of the transcript that the girl herself
could not or would not recall it
and then describes her as a survivor

Which of course is from the Latin
meaning to live on
to outlive others

I would not have used that word

The Skeleton of a Trout in Shallow Water

wedged between two stones
near the bank of a rushing stream
startled the old man with the shock
of white hair who uncovered it
while stooping to pick watercress.
For a long time he examined the skeleton—
skull, ribs, and spine polished clean—
before dislodging it with his cane
and watching it spin away
into the fast current
and disappear through the shadows
of the overhanging trees.
Then, with the sun beating down
on his head and bleaching
the fields that stretched away
to the mountains, he released
the dripping clump of watercress
he had been clutching all that time
and watched it float away, too,
dark and tangled in the clear water.

After a Long Illness

A man lighter than air enters
the glass house, switches on
every lamp, and turns the radio
to a station broadcasting
the sound of birds' wings flapping
skyward over a deep lake at dawn.

He pours himself a glass of water
from a tall pitcher on which
a crane, drinking from a pitcher,
has been etched in the enamel.
He makes a sandwich of brightly colored
pieces of paper and slices it in half.

Opening a window, he reels in
a clothesline with two billowing
sheets, white as ocean clouds,
and lays them on a bed so high
he would need a ladder to reach it
were he not lighter than air.

He reclines on the bed with a book
of photographs of birds in flight
and gazes up through the glass roof
at the full moon and the stars.
In the morning, a quart of milk
is left at the door, a letter is

dropped through the mail slot,
the lawn is mowed and the shrubs
trimmed, but there is no one home.
A woman arrives in a see-through
raincoat, switches off the lamps
and the radio, climbs to the roof,
. . . . .

and lets out a kite on a long string.
Winding the string in hours later,
she finds it attached, not to the kite,
but to a man who is fast asleep,
trailing vapors, his arms folded
across his chest like wings.

Funeral Parlor, Trieste

The man in the broken-
brimmed hat turns into
the glare of a 40-watt
bulb to see the body
of his mother, his eyelids
fluttering like moths.

This side of the windowpane
is as cold as the outside.
The wind from the sea blows
right through the room—
we can feel it, ruffling our
cuffs, but we can't hear it.

On the dusty table the scent
of the roses in the cheap
vase is faintly metallic.
In the cut-glass ashtray
a thread of smoke rises
from a cigarette, its filter
ringed with lipstick

the color of fresh blood.
But no one in the room smokes,
and the only woman present
is dead. Her face powdered
whiter than the falling snow.
Some chairs are lined up
before a brown curtain.

Behind the curtain someone
is pouring water into a glass.
The ice cubes are clinking
sharply. I'm thirsty, too.
Then, somewhere above us,
a door opens and closes.

. . . . .

And in the basement, where
they prepare the bodies,
a man coughs, and another
man laughs—mechanically—
as if he was told a joke
he'd heard many times before.

After Hours

The man who mops the floor of the luncheonette
at 2 A.M. when everyone's gone home is talking
to himself again, puffing a cigarette, listening
to Christmas carols on the radio, and pausing
before the calendar pinup that the cook has taped
below his chopping block (a wide-eyed woman wearing
only a pink cowboy hat, holster, and six-guns) while
computing the amount of cash he will have left over
from his paycheck after seeing to his rent, utilities,
and such incidentals as the payment on his late
wife's hospital bills and the installment on his
car that no longer starts (what's left will be eleven
dollars to underwrite his pack-a-day of cigarettes
and a lottery ticket)—all the while continuing
to mop the floor, around the stools, between booths,
under tables, into the rest rooms, the harsh ammonia
fumes from the pail biting into the back of his throat.

Sometimes, on nights like this, when the moon
has risen over the office buildings, and the sharp
wind is rattling the cages on the storefronts,
and the freshly fallen snow has not yet been blackened
by rush-hour traffic, he locks up the luncheonette,
puts up his collar, and takes the long way around to
the subway. Past the public park with the Civil War
general stiff on horseback and the pigeons huddled
sleeping in the trees. Past warehouses where icicles,
like stalactites, drip from gutters eight stories up.
Down by the river for a single block, where he can gaze
along the path the moonlight follows to the opposite
shore—the murk of barges, wharves, and factories,
the rusted freighters, illuminated for an instant like
the blue panes in a stained-glass window that depicts
a redemption scene—before he completes his detour,
turning back into the darkness, the iron stairwell to
the subway on which his heavy boots do not make a sound.

The Hotel Miramar

In the cabana, their hair twisted with brine,
the bride and groom sipped wine from iced tumblers.

Reflecting the moon's rays, her quartz eyes lit up
the volcanic stone dangling from his neck.

Musicians in snowy jackets swayed, their instruments
gleaming, on waves that never rolled to shore.

They played softly, into the wind, but the sound
carried far down the beach, to the village where

brightly colored fish were stuck like bits
of paper in the drift nets hung out to dry.

When a thunderclap broke on the horizon,
all the stars in the sky fell hissing into the sea.

Through the windows of the hotel, instead of
rooms, corridors, and guests, a mountain was visible.

Densely green, with vines that slid up the trees
like snakes, it was blanketed with steam.

Wildcats wrestled on its sheer cliffs.
Birds flew in and out of its waterfalls.

When a pair of these birds glided down
to the beach and coupled in midair,

two cries were heard from the cabana in rapid
succession, followed by a sudden downpour.

Through which the band continued to play
while the stars floated up beneath their feet.

Angel's Bakery

A dusty fan blows the smell
of hot bread into the black drizzle.
Through sooty windows nothing
but shadows are visible,
white in their hats and aprons,
moving as if underwater
to the strains of *Don Giovanni*
from a radio tucked among the ovens.
In the truck at the loading zone
the driver is slumped behind the wheel
with his cap pulled low.
His hands white as flour.
His chest so still he could be dead.
On the side of the building
there is a mural of Angel
faded by the elements.
She is young, with braided hair
the color of wheat and a sly smile.
A golden halo frames her head.
A boy with sweat pouring off
his temples wheels a cart
of bread out the corrugated door
and replies to anyone who inquires,
"There never was an Angel,"
as rain hisses on the steaming
loaves and the driver snaps awake,
gunning the truck's engine.

The First Day of Spring

Smoking a clove cigarette from Java
(seaside palms pictured on the tin)
and painting a cane chair sky-blue
I'm perched on the edge of the bathtub
under the rubber plant that nearly
obscures the frosted window
when a shaft of sunlight penetrates
the floppy leaves and strikes the nape
of my neck with such intensity
that all at once vistas open before me
of snow swirling at the polar caps
and mist boiling up from equatorial jungles
and this same sun that is alighting
on my neck scorching a desert
where a lone traveler in search of water
has just glanced up at the sky
and discovered that he is blind

The Palm Reader

In her storefront living room—
overstuffed couch, oversized TV, a bowl of mints
on the Plexiglas coffee table—
she watches *Edge of Night* and files her nails.
The paraphernalia pertaining to her trade
crowd a shelf beneath the large green hand
painted onto the window: a Tarot deck,
coins and obelisks, a chalky bust with numbered
phrenological divisions on the skull.
Through the beaded curtain in the rear
some clues emerge as to *her* life:
two children trading insults,
a man calling out, "Eggs!"
as a frying pan clatters into a sink,
a dog running by with a wig in his mouth.
She herself is plump, heavily made up,
wearing a red dress and a shawl imprinted
with the signs of the zodiac.
A gold pyramid hangs from her throat
and she has combed glittering
silver stars through her black hair.
From a plush rocker she beckons you,
at the window, to a straight-back chair
in which she will divine (according to the sign
on the door) "the roads into your future,
and helpful information from the Beyond."
Though the latter, especially, tempts
you powerfully, you decline,
and she shrugs with a rueful smile.
And because it is close to noon,
and the sidewalk is empty, as you cross
the street she closes up for lunch.
Her living room in which matters of life
and death—of human destiny laid bare—
suddenly reverts to its other function:
husband slumped on the couch clutching a beer,

children sopping bread across paper plates,
the dog sprawled under the table.
All of them watching *Edge of Night* now.
The fate of whose characters, which keeps
a faithful public tuning in day after day,
year after year, is presumably known
to this woman, lighting a cigarette
and surveying that room, open to all passersby
yet utterly remote, as inescapable
as the future itself, that jumps out
at her from every stranger's hand.

When the Hurricane Swerved Toward the Island

a radio began playing through the forest
where it was always night
and the thin trunks of the bamboo trees
clicked together like hundreds of clocks ticking

There were no houses beyond that forest
just the burned-out church
in which the high grass glowed like moonlight
and ghosts lined the broken pews sipping darkness

And beyond the church miles of scorched sugarcane
and fields of jagged boulders
and hidden valleys to which the tropicbirds descended
from the mountains without once beating their wings

Until that moment on my terrace overlooking the bay
many sounds had drifted from the forest
the squawking of toucans and the cries of the cats
and the insects' staccato clatter but never a radio

And now it drowned out everything else
first with a snatch of music which kept changing keys
and then a voice swimming in static and not altogether human
that tried to reach us from across the sea

Your Father's Ghost

Turning a corner uptown, I crossed paths
with a man in a long gray coat.
I recognized his profile, blurred by
the fast-falling snow, as he hurried off.

At a stand-up counter, behind windows
steamed white by the customers' breath,
I sidled up and ordered a cup of coffee.
The man was eating a slice of lemon pie.

Reflected in a grimy mirror, a woman was
rattling through the contents of her purse.
Her eyeliner was green as a leaf.
She was wearing gloves embroidered with swans.

The man walked out, paying with foreign
coins, while the woman put a cigarette
between her lips and, without lighting it,
blew smoke rings up to the ceiling fan.

The man entered a taxi whose driver
had one arm, one eye, and one ear.
The taxi itself only had wheels on one side,
and it sped around the corner on them.

That night, in a hotel on the river,
I opened the window wide and drew
the frigid air deep into my lungs.
Then I had that dream again.

The one in which I attend a funeral
in an icy field, on a clear day, and hear
someone singing in the nearby birch forest.
A girl is clutching yellow flowers.
. . . . .

The undertakers are trying in vain
to break ground with picks and shovels.
And a man who has just climbed out of his
coffin is brushing the snow from his coat.

Bees

1.

With three hundred lenses in each eye
a worker bee gazes on the same glass
skyscraper six hundred times
from the blossom of a solitary tree

2.

During a solar eclipse all the bees
from a single hive stop
flying at the same instant
and cluster low to the ground

3.

In the chapter of the Koran entitled "The Bee"
they receive a single passing verse praising
their honey ("a syrup of different hues")
as a cure for the myriad maladies men incur

4.

A girl on the island of Naxos was stung
over her entire body in a rainstorm
in December (when bees hibernate) and for
a hundred years could prophesy the future

5.

When Benvenuto Cellini was imprisoned in Rome
he dreamt of bees swarming the head of a woman
on a golden staircase and this became the *Medusa*
(with bees instead of snakes)
he cast in gold for the Duke of Parma
who placed it on a pedestal opposite his bed
where it remained gazing at him
(& emitting a low hum) until the day of his death

A Storm

It's raining cats and dogs.
And did you know that "vindaloo" (as in
Shrimp Vindaloo) is not an Indian word at all,
but a pidgin slurring of the Portuguese
for "wine of garlic"?

There is a film I have otherwise forgotten
(but not the makeshift cinema in which I viewed it:
a converted bakery storeroom on the island of Spetses)
that ended with the line:
"If no one escaped drowning, who are these strangers?"

What we will never know,
watching this cold sky turn on its invisible axis,
is how much punishment you have absorbed—
you, the victim of crimes, and you, the criminal—
for a set of principles no one can remember.

The rain on our lips is fiery with spices.
We are hurrying along a tangle of slick streets,
up blind alleys and through hidden archways,
the wind whipping our coats,
to an appointment we should not keep.
The words on the scrap of paper crumpled in your hand
      confirm this.

Before the night began to run like ink,
engulfing everyone who had no place to hide,
a woman with a beautiful voice was cooking for us
without questions or reservations
in a kitchen that glowed orange.

In that film, it was just such a voice—
but frightened—that delivered the last line.
Also in a city whose streets had no end.
Also while rats scratched about in the darkness,
as in the bakery's storeroom.

. . . . .

Still searching for crumbs where there could be none.
The story of someone else's life
which nevertheless must infringe on our own,
until it furiously alters the facts we had stored up
and polished for so many years.

On that scrap of paper is also a telephone number
you misdialed, which has sent us off in the wrong direction.
Something an impartial observer, watching us zigzag,
might ascribe to fate before growing nervous
and asking someone at the edge of the crowd,
"If no one escaped drowning, who are these strangers?"

Far from Home

A broken-down hotel on an inhospitable sea,
and behind it, a field of thorns in which
a man wearing white gloves is digging a hole
with the exact proportions of a grave.

Down the hall, the young chambermaid
is staring into a basin full of red water.
Her hair is white and her hands are wrinkled.
A shark tooth dangles from her ear.

In the evening she leaves a tray by my door:
a glass, a carafe of water, and a bottle
containing liquor that swirls like mist.
Mornings she brings bitter tea and a map.

Always the same map—not of the island
we're on, but of one I left long ago.
(If it were this island, I wouldn't know,
having never ventured from the hotel.)

There is a bowl of black seashells by my bed.
The maps—thirteen of them—are stacked
between the lamp that flickers like a star
and the quartz lions veined with light.

The clerk at the front desk could be a statue.
His dark glasses reflect the bare lobby,
its leafless plants and shuttered windows.
At his fingertips is a tumbler filled with dust.

The day I check out, the other guests line
the balcony, wrapped in sheets, speaking
a language I've never heard—sibilant as
the sea, but with no two words sounding alike.
. . . . .

The man in white gloves appears, to carry
my suitcase, and pauses before a mirror
in which I see, not his image, but towering
iron waves, rising to mesh with an iron sky.

Cornelia Street, 6 A.M.

I'm buying hot bread
from a woman with fingerless
gloves and a harsh cough.
Snow is falling fast
and the sidewalk over
the bakery's basement
ovens is steaming.
The proprietor of the fish
store is leaning in his
doorway, hands on hips,
with fish blood smeared
across his apron.
The off-duty detective
enters the coffee shop
and removes his coat,
revealing the .38
revolver that is licensed
to take human life in
the defense of human life.
A man walking a pair
of dogs is peering through
his own reflection
in the pawnshop window
at a broken violin.
Four stories up, light-years
away from all of this,
a woman who hasn't slept
in days stands by an open
window tearing a letter
into tiny pieces which
blow out into the snow,
indistinguishable from
the snow, and melt the moment
they touch the street.

Five Shades of Purple

I was reading in the dark in a hotel room
from a book the previous occupant
or his predecessor
or a guest far more remote
had left in the desk drawer beneath a spider's web
to be discovered by generations of transients

Through the broken slats of the shutters
pierced by needles of starlight
the desert's red and blue shadows
like ink merged into shades of purple
of varying intensity
one for every hour I would not sleep

I sipped from a glass of ice water
in which the cubes made no sound
and then tossed fitfully on the rough sheets
retracing across the ceiling the zigzag route
I had followed for weeks with a handful
of detailed and contradictory maps

The book was *The Orchard* by Saadi
a thirteenth-century Sufi and at dawn I put it
back in the drawer and by noon when I checked out
a spider had spun a web over it and only a single line
from its pages remained in my head darkly lit
I have never seen a man lost who was on a straight path

Railroad Bridge

A woman is running along the tracks,
trailing a scarf, clutching a suitcase.
Every ten yards, she passes through a cone
of light, freezing her in motion for an instant
before she merges back into the darkness.
Darting in and out of sight like that,
many times, as she heads toward the lone tree,
shining like iron, that stands beneath
a streetlight at the foot of the bridge.
It is there that the overnight express will
rush in from the east, caked with dirty snow,
and send the pigeons flying from the trestle.
So that all at once the brief shadows
of their wings will be swallowed up
by the river below, the jagged water silvering
at the edges while the train whistle screams.

Assignation After Attending a Funeral

A clear spring night
and the cool wind is filling my shirt,
rushing in the sleeves darkly
and encircling me
as a bat glides over the steeple
where the clock lit up bright green
has no hands, no face.

May Day, 1992

Los Angeles is burning tonight.
Here in New York
there is a new moon, black in the sky,
that we cannot see.
The president is on the television
hung high above the bar—
above the rows of bottles in strict formation—
where men hunched over are drinking
dark drinks from small glasses.
He is wearing a black suit.
His face is wizened, his eyes unblinking,
as he speaks from behind a sheet
of pale water that flickers.
He could be far away, in space,
or on the floor of the sea.
The sound on the television is turned off,
but I know what he's saying.
I've come in to use the pay phone,
where a woman in lizard boots
and a vinyl skirt has the receiver
nestled beneath her wig.
She signals me for a light—
for the cigarette that has materialized
between her fingers out of nowhere.
I have no light.
She hangs up and strolls back down the bar.
I dial my own phone number,
but the line is busy;
I try again, and lose my quarter.
The president is still speaking.
His expression has not changed,
his hands are folded on his desk.
On the subway platform at Columbus Circle
two men in sunglasses
with a crackling portable speaker
at their feet are alternately

shouting into the microphone—
a kind of dialogue—
echoing the same line
back & forth, over & over:
Baby, run, that's what I say!
Sweat is pouring off their brows.
One of them is wearing a necklace
of gold-plated shark's teeth.
The other has a watch
on a long elastic band
fastened around his head,
centered above the nose.
It has no hands to tell the time.
Baby, run, that's what I say
Up above, the streets are too quiet.
Occasional sirens, and motorcycles backfiring.
And a faint, acrid, early-spring scent—
like gunpowder, or perfume.
The express roars in and I can
still hear the two men
shouting, back & forth,
as we pull out of the station.
Downtown, a phalanx of cops
in riot gear is patrolling
8th Street, where even the 24-hour
papaya stand is shut up tight,
its orange neon sign—
HOT DOGS 60¢ ALL BEEF
not blinking for once
and no one in sight anywhere.
Inside the appliance store
one of the televisions
has been left on in the window,
behind the security cage,
and the president is just finishing
his speech, his face and hands

like white stone, so far away,
and still I can't hear him
but I know what he's saying.
Then the screen goes blank
and Los Angeles appears,
an aerial view in which whole
blocks are burning fiercely,
and a woman with red hair comes on
to discuss what the president said.
Baby, run, that's what I say

Hanalei Valley

A solitary horse is grazing in grass
that reaches to his shoulders.
A white egret is perched on his back,
reflected in the river that flows
past them without a ripple.
Enormous clouds span the sky.
In the deep stillness it seems as if the earth
has stopped rotating on its axis.
Then the egret takes flight,
rising in a long arc with its slow-beating wings
against the lush, green mountains
where it rains day and night,
where it is raining even now
as I write this,
as you read it.

1960

Playing hide-and-seek at dusk.
Just the two of us, for an hour, where the blue trees,
heavy with foliage, grow in parallel rows.
Wind rushing the clouds north.
Stars glinting like nicks on smoked glass.

In this maze of tree trunks straight as pillars
it should not be difficult to find a girl
with long hair, in a pale dress, who is clutching
a jar of fireflies as she darts through shadows,
surefooted on the slippery grass.

But even before the night flows in around me
from the lake, cold as the deepest water
in the lake, and I strain my eyes
and listen closely for the faintest sound,
I know she is someone I will never find.

Kismet, Paradise, and El Dorado

are small towns in Kansas which, if connected
with three lines, form an equilateral triangle—
half of a square within the larger rectangle of Kansas itself—
that lies at the exact midpoint of the continent.
To drive the dusty roads through the golden wheat
fields from one of those towns to the next,
following the triangle as closely as possible,

along Routes 54, 35, 19, 18, and then back to 54—
their numbers adding up to 180, the number of degrees
in a triangle—offers rewards that depend on
where you start and which direction you first take.
Paradise, to the north, ought to be the logical destination,
a place in which to linger blissfully, while El Dorado,
with its capacity to fulfill (or dash) our dreams of
riches, should best be seen as a way station (or detour).

Which leaves Kismet—"fate"—as the point of departure,
as it is for all of us, Kansans or otherwise,
when at birth (or even some later date),
with or without the luxury of straight lines to travel,
we're dropped someplace, in the middle of something,
where we can survey the horizon in all directions
and chart our positions, but not our fate.

The State Hospital, Honolulu

The nurse is sitting with crossed legs and crossed
arms on a stone bench among the oleander shrubs.
Light streams from a single window on the hospital's

top floor, casting a yellow rectangle on the lawn.
Later, a priest will be silhouetted in that window,
adminstering the last rites to a blind girl.

The nurse has been mesmerized by Mercury and the Moon
moving in conjunction, until the planet, like a topaz
chip, settles within the curve of the Moon's sickle.

The red blossoms and nectar of the oleander (member
of the dogbane family) are so toxic even the insects
avoid them; its wood, on a cooking fire, is poisonous.

Someone planted oleanders around these grounds in
1910, when the first hospital was built—the one
that burned to the ground forty years later.

Sixty patients were killed, and four nurses died
on the first floor, inhaling the oleanders' smoke.
Even so, when the hospital was rebuilt, oleanders were

planted in the same plots, ringing the granite walls.
The nurse glances at the luminous dial of her watch,
the green of some planet invisible to the naked eye.

In her handbag is the sandwich she wrapped in foil
at dawn, mint wafers, and a black plum, but she is
not hungry tonight. She combs out her hair and one

of those blossoms drops into her lap, brushing her lips
as it falls. Then she lights a cigarette and blows halos
of smoke up over the palms. And when mist seeps through
. . . . .

the iron fence and swirls around her ankles, she feels
as if she has stepped out of her body and is studying
it from afar, on that stone bench where she will remain

forever, wasting away to a skeleton, to dust, while her
watch dial glows an even brighter green, and the rectangle
of light on the lawn receives her, like a grave.

About the Author

Nicholas Christopher was born in 1951, and was graduated from Harvard College. He has published four previous books of poems, the most recent of which, *In the Year of the Comet* (Viking Penguin, 1992), was awarded the Melville Cane Award from the Poetry Society of America as "the best book of poems by an American poet in 1992–93." His other books are *Desperate Characters: A Novella in Verse & Other Poems* (1988) and *A Short History of the Island of Butterflies* (1986), also published by Viking Penguin, and *On Tour with Rita* (Knopf, 1982). He is the author of two novels, *The Soloist* (Viking, 1986) and *Veronica*, forthcoming from the Dial Press, and he edited the anthologies *Walk on the Wild Side: Urban American Poetry Since 1975* (Scribner's/Collier, 1994) and *Under 35: The New Generation of American Poets* (Anchor, 1989). He is the recipient of numerous other awards, including poetry fellowships from the National Endowment for the Arts and the New York Foundation for the Arts, the Amy Lowell Poetry Travelling Fellowship, the Peter I.B. Lavan Younger Poets Award from the Academy of American Poets, and a Fellowship in Poetry from the John Simon Guggenheim Memorial Foundation for 1993–94. He has published his work widely in leading magazines and in various anthologies in the United States and abroad. He lives in New York City.

Some of the poems in this book first appeared in the following publications:

Columbia Magazine: "5°: 15.," "May Day, 1992"
Grand Street: "5°: 14., 16., 24."
The Nation: "5°: 18.," "A Storm," "The State Hospital, Honolulu"
The New Republic: "Hibiscus Tea," "Funeral Parlor, Trieste," "The Hotel
    Miramar," "Angel's Bakery"
The New Yorker: "5°: 1.," "The Quiñero Sisters, 1968," "The Skeleton of a
    Trout in Shallow Water"
The Ontario Review: "Bees," "Far from Home," "Cornelia Street, 6 A.M.,"
    "Railroad Bridge"
The Paris Review: "5°: 5., 6., 7., 10., 11., 13., 22.," "Terminus"
Poetry: "5°: 17.," "After a Long Illness"
Western Humanities Review: "The First Day of Spring"